Scan the QR code
to read and listen to the
glossary words for FREE!

glossary - Meanings of words.

Every Cherry Publishing, an imprint of Sweet Cherry Publishing Limited.

Published in the UK by Sweet Cherry Publishing Limited, 2024
Unit 36, Vulcan House, Vulcan Road,
Leicester, LE5 3EF, United Kingdom

Nauschgasse 4/3/2 POB 1017
Vienna, WI 1220, Austria

SWEET CHERRY and EVERY CHERRY and associated logos
are trademarks and/or registered trademarks of
Sweet Cherry Publishing Limited.

2 4 6 8 10 9 7 5 3 1

ISBN: 978-1-80263-335-1

© Sweet Cherry Publishing Limited, 2024

Football Rising Stars: Marcus Rashford
Easier Edition

Original text by Harry Meredith.
Adapted for easier reading by Every Cherry.
Internal illustrations by Ludovic Sallé.

All rights reserved. No part of this publication may be
reproduced or utilised in any form or by any means, electronic
or mechanical, including photocopying, recording, or using
any information storage and retrieval system, without prior
permission in writing from the publisher.

www.everycherry.com

Printed and bound in China

Every Cherry

MARCUS RASHFORD
THE UNOFFICIAL STORY

Written by
HARRY MEREDITH

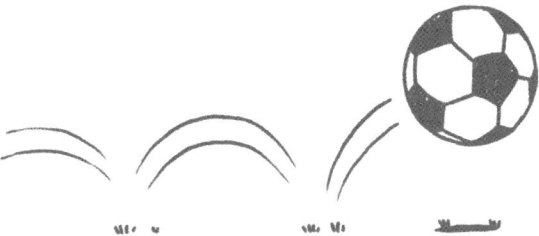

Every Cherry Easier Edition

Meet the Characters

Marcus Rashford

José Mourinho

Phil Jones

Mission Impossible

Manchester United were playing Paris Saint-Germain, in the **knock-out stage** of the **Champions League**.

Manchester United had lost 0-2 to Paris Saint-Germain in their first game. They had to fight hard to win this game so they could stay in the competition.

The last player onto the field was Manchester United's Marcus Rashford.

knock-out stage - The second part of a football competition where teams are no longer allowed to play if they lose the game.

Champions League - A yearly football competition between the best European football clubs.

Quickly, both teams scored.

Then, Marcus shot the ball towards the net. It hit the goalkeeper, but then another teammate kicked the ball again and scored!

With minutes left, Manchester United got a **penalty**. Marcus stepped forward to take it. He scored!

Manchester United won 3-1!

penalty - A free kick given to a team when the other team breaks the rules.

Who is Marcus Rashford?

Marcus Rashford was born on the 31st of October 1997.

He is the youngest of five children, all raised by his single mum, Melanie Maynard.

His family didn't have a lot of money and sometimes couldn't buy food. But even though they were poor, Marcus's family supported his love of football.

Even at seven years old, Marcus was very **skilled** at football.

Growing up, Marcus played for a football club called the Fletcher Moss Rangers. In an important competition, Marcus scored twelve goals!

Scouts from Manchester United saw him playing. They thought Marcus was so **skilled** that they invited him to come and train at their **football academy**!

skilled - Doing a task very well.

Scouts - Someone who goes to football games to find players for their teams.

football academy - A football school for young football players who want to get better at football.

Manchester United Academy

Marcus did very well in his first few years at the academy. He was quickly becoming an amazing footballer.

For boys between 12 and 16 years old, there was a **scholarship programme** called Manchester United Schoolboy Scholars Scheme.

Since Marcus was only 11, he wasn't sure if he could join the programme.

scholarship programme - Money given by a school to a student to pay for them to learn.

But because of Marcus's amazing skills and his family's struggles with money, he was allowed to join early.

Now he was going to have to leave his home and school to focus on football at the academy.

On the day he moved into his new house, he found out that famous footballers had lived there too. His **idols** had lived in that very house!

idols - People who are liked a lot because of their actions or skills.

A Life-Changing Three Days

At 18 years old, Marcus was such a talented player that he was chosen for the **first team**!

In the **Europa League**, Marcus was a **substitute**. But when his teammate got injured, Marcus got to play against FC Midtjylland.

In the game, Marcus scored two goals! Manchester United won!

first team - The highest level team in a club.

Europa League - A yearly football competition between European football teams.

substitute - An extra player who might replace another player during a game.

Two days later, Marcus was chosen for the Manchester United **Premier League** team.

They were playing against Arsenal, one of Manchester United's biggest **rivals**. In the 29th minute, Marcus scored a goal. Then, three minutes later, he scored again!

Manchester United won! The fans stood and cheered for Marcus!

Premier League - The highest level football league in England and Wales.
rivals - A team that another team finds hard to win against or doesn't like very much.

Fight for the FA Cup

After Marcus's first game with Manchester United, he became a member of the team.

He was now a **professional footballer!**

Marcus got to join the Manchester United team in the **FA Cup**. He helped them to win the **semi-finals**.

Manchester United were going to the **FA Cup** final!

professional footballer - Someone who plays football for their job.

FA Cup - A competition held every year between English and Welsh football teams.

semi-finals - The part in a competition where four teams are left.

On the 16th of May 2016, Manchester United played in the FA Cup final against Crystal Palace.

In the second half, Marcus crashed into another player and fell to the floor. Then, a Crystal Palace player lost his balance and stood on Marcus's knee.

Marcus was hurt and couldn't finish the game! He had to watch the rest of the game from the **sidelines**.

sidelines - The white or sometimes coloured lines that show where a playing field starts and ends.

Not long after he had left, Crystal Palace scored a goal. But Manchester United scored a goal of their own soon after.

The game was drawn and neither team could score before the 90 minutes were up so the game went into **extra time**.

Luckily, Manchester United scored another goal! Manchester United had won the FA Cup!

extra time - The time added on at the end of a game when the two teams are drawn and one team has to win.

National Team Dreams

As the 2015 to 2016 Premier League season came to an end, Marcus kept training as best as he could.

At the end of a team training session, Phil Jones, his teammate, came to **congratulate** Marcus for getting into the England team.

Marcus was surprised and thought Phil was joking. So, Marcus went to check his phone.

congratulate - To praise someone when something good has happened to them.

Marcus had a new message on his phone. It was a list of all the new England team players and his name was on it!

Marcus couldn't believe it! He was going to be playing for the England team!

Marcus flew to France to play in the 2016 **European Championship**. England were playing Iceland in the knock-out stage.

European Championship - *A yearly football competition between European teams. It is also known as the Euros.*

Everyone thought that England were the better team and were going to win.

But Iceland played well during the game. They scored two goals, and England only scored one.

England were knocked out of the competition by Iceland!

José Mourinho

When Marcus arrived back to Manchester United, he had a new team manager called José Mourinho.

José was a very famous and successful manager. He had trained teams all over the world and had led them to win many games.

José was sure that Marcus's skills would bring great things to the team.

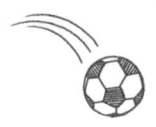

José taught Marcus that he didn't need to score lots of goals to be a good footballer.

Marcus also learnt how to deal with losing.

The team didn't do very well during the season, and Marcus didn't get to score as many goals as usual. But José believed that Marcus was a winner and taught Marcus all that he could.

Europa League Battle

In 2017, Manchester United made it all the way to the final of the Europa League. They were playing the Dutch team Ajax.

Marcus and his team played well. With one goal from Paul Pogba and another from Chris Smalling, Manchester United won!

Next, Manchester United had the 2017 to 2018 Premier League to play.

Manchester United played so well that they finished second place in the league. Although, they were sad to lose to Manchester City, they were proud of their achievements that season.

Marcus had played much better throughout the league, scoring seven goals.

But Marcus didn't have time to relax afterwards. Instead, he was picked for the English **World Cup** team!

World Cup - A competition that happens every four years between football teams from all over the world.

World Cup 2018

Marcus and the England team arrived in Russia for the 2018 World Cup.

After getting through the **group stage**, they went into the knock-out stage of the competition.

They were playing Colombia, another strong team. In the first half of the game, neither team could score.

group stage - The first part of a football competition. Teams are split into groups and play every team in their group. The team with the most wins moves onto the next stage.

In the 57th minute, England got a penalty when an England player was dragged to the ground by a Colombian defender. Harry Kane stepped up to take the shot. He scored!

But in the final few minutes of the game, Colombia scored too!

The game went into extra time. Both teams played well, but neither could score.

The winner was going to be decided by a **penalty shoot-out**. After every player had taken their shot, England had won! They went through to the **quarter-finals**!

In the **quarter-finals**, England beat Sweden 2-0. But sadly, they lost to Croatia 1-2 in the semi-finals.

Even though they didn't win the World Cup, Marcus and his teammates came home as heroes.

penalty shoot-out - A way to decide the winning team if no one scores in extra time. Players take turns shooting at the goal until one team wins.

quarter-finals - The part in a competition where eight teams are left.

Solskjær's Return

*Manchester United played badly in the 2018 to 2019 Premier League. They even got knocked out of the **League Cup** by Derby County!*

Because the team kept losing, José Mourinho was fired.

Ole Gunnar Solskjær became the new manager. He used to play for Manchester United and was a very skilled footballer!

League Cup - *A yearly football competition between English and Welsh football teams. It is now known as the Carabao Cup.*

With Solskjær as manager, the team became happier and more energetic. Manchester United started to win games again!

Solskjær used to play in the same position Marcus played in, so Marcus learnt a lot from him.

By the end of the Premier League season, Marcus had scored 10 goals and 7 **assists**!

assists - When a football player helps another player to score a goal.

Marcus Rashford's Award

In 2020, the UK went into **lockdown** because of the **COVID-19 global pandemic**.

Football stadiums became empty, schools shut down and everyone stayed inside.

Marcus began working with a **charity** to give food to poor families. He helped give meals to 3 million people around the country.

lockdown - When no one is allowed to go outside in order to keep them safe.
COVID-19 global pandemic - A sickness that spread across the whole world in 2020.
charity - A company that gives money and help to people who need it.

One morning, Marcus saw on the news that free school meals were cancelled over the summer holidays because of the pandemic.

When Marcus was young, he needed free school meals to get enough food.

So, Marcus wrote a letter to the government and posted it on social media. The UK's Prime Minister read the letter and thought that Marcus was right.

The government was going to make sure children could get food over the summer.

Because of Marcus's work helping feed children during the pandemic, he was given an **MBE** *by Queen Elizabeth II!*

MBE - An award given to a person by the king or queen of the UK for a high achievement.

European Championship 2020

When the pandemic was over, Marcus was chosen for the England team in the 2020 European Championship.

After beating Croatia and the Czech Republic and drawing with Scotland, England were through to the knock-out stage.

They were playing Germany. In the last 15 minutes of the game, England scored twice and won!

England faced Ukraine in the quarter-finals and beat them 4-0.

England's semi-final against Denmark was harder. Both teams could only manage to score one goal by the end of the 90 minutes. But in extra time, England scored again!

England found themselves in their first ever European Championship final! They were playing Italy.

Early in the final, England scored! But Italy scored a goal of their own in the second half. Neither team scored again, so the winner had to be decided by a penalty shoot-out.

Marcus was the third penalty taker. He was very **nervous**. He kicked the ball and missed the goal! Then, two other England players missed their penalties.

England lost the final.

nervous - When someone feels scared or worried.

Becoming a Hero

After the European Championship, Marcus went home and spent time with his family and friends.

Marcus wanted to continue his work to give children food who needed it most, just like he had done during the pandemic.

So he decided to help at a local **food bank.**

food bank - A place where people with not much money can go to get food for free.

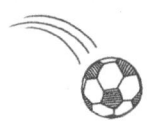

As Marcus stepped into the food bank, the volunteers cheered and thanked him for all of his support.

But Marcus didn't want them to thank him. The people helping to run the food bank were the real heroes to him.

Marcus went to the playground at the back of the food bank. All of the children were excited to see him and he took photos with all of them.

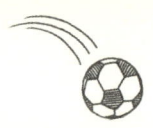

When Marcus was a little boy, he dreamt of being a famous footballer. Now that he was one, he knew that he had to use his fame to help others.

Even though Marcus had lots more money and was famous now, he would never forget what it was like to have no money.

He now uses his fame and money to help those who need it.

HARRY MEREDITH

Harry Meredith writes stories for children. He studied in England and the USA! Harry loves football, and when he's not watching games, he's writing and heading out on adventures!

Coming soon ...

Kylian Mbappé: The Unofficial Story

Football Rising Stars

Harry Meredith

Every Cherry Easier Edition

Visit our website to learn more:
www.everycherry.com